LOP

D0997025

TELL ME SOMETHING HAPPY BEFORE I GO TO SLEEP
A DOUBLEDAY BOOK 0 385 60499 8

Published in Great Britain by Doubleday,
an imprint of Random House Children's Books

First published by Doubleday in 1998
This mini abridged edition published 2002

1 3 5 7 9 10 8 6 4 2

Text copyright © Joyce Dunbar 1998
Illustrations copyright © Debi Gliori 1998
Designed by Ian Butterworth

The right of Joyce Dunbar to be identified as the author of this work and the right of Debi Gliori to be identified as
the illustrator of this work has been asserted in accordance with the Copyright, Designs and Patents Act 1988

All rights reserved. No part of this publication may be reproduced, stored in a retrieval system,
or transmitted in any form or by any means, electronic, mechanical, photocopying, recording or otherwise,
without the prior permission of the publishers.

RANDOM HOUSE CHILDREN'S BOOKS
61-63 Uxbridge Rd, London W5 5SA
A division of The Random House Group Ltd.

RANDOM HOUSE AUSTRALIA (PTY) LTD
20 Alfred Street, Milsons Point, Sydney,
New South Wales 2061, Australia

RANDOM HOUSE NEW ZEALAND LTD
18 Poland Road, Glenfield, Auckland 10, New Zealand

RANDOM HOUSE (PTY) LTD
Endulini, 5A Jubilee Road, Parktown 2193, South Africa

THE RANDOM HOUSE GROUP Limited Reg. No. 954009
www.kidsatrandomhouse.co.uk

A CIP catalogue record for this book is available from the British Library.

Printed in Hong Kong by Midas Printing International Ltd

Tell Me Something Happy

Before I Go to Sleep

Joyce Dunbar · Debi Gliori

DOUBLEDAY

Willa was tired,
so Willa went to bed.

She lay with her pillow this way...
...and that way.
But Willa couldn't sleep.

"Willoughby," called Willa.
"Are you there?"
"Yes," answered Willoughby.
"I'm here."
"I can't sleep," said Willa.
"Why can't you sleep?"
asked Willoughby.
"I'm afraid that I might
have a bad dream,"
said Willa.
"Think of something happy,
then you won't have
a bad dream,"
said Willoughby.

So Willa tried to think of something happy,
but she couldn't.
"Willoughby," called Willa. "Are you
still there?"

"Yes," answered Willoughby.
"I'm still here."
"You tell me. Tell me something happy
before I go to sleep."

Willoughby thought for a moment.
Then he said,
"Willa, look under your bed."

So Willa leaned over and looked under the bed.

"What do you see?" asked Willoughby.

"I see my chicken slippers," said Willa.

"That's right," said Willoughby. "And your slippers are
waiting, just waiting, for nobody's feet but yours."
"Good," said Willa. "That's happy. What else?"

"What do you see on the chair?"
asked Willoughby.
"I see my blue and white jumpsuit," said Willa.
"That's right," said Willoughby. "And your jumpsuit
is longing, just longing, for
tomorrow, when you will jump
out of bed to put it on."
"Good," said Willa. "That's
happy. What else?"

Willoughby picked Willa up in his arms and padded softly downstairs to the kitchen. He opened the larder door.

"Do you see the bread and honey and oats and milk and apples?" asked Willoughby.
"Yes," said Willa.
"Lovely food! All waiting to be made into breakfast, for you and me to share," said Willoughby.
"Oh good," said Willa.
"That's happy. What else?"

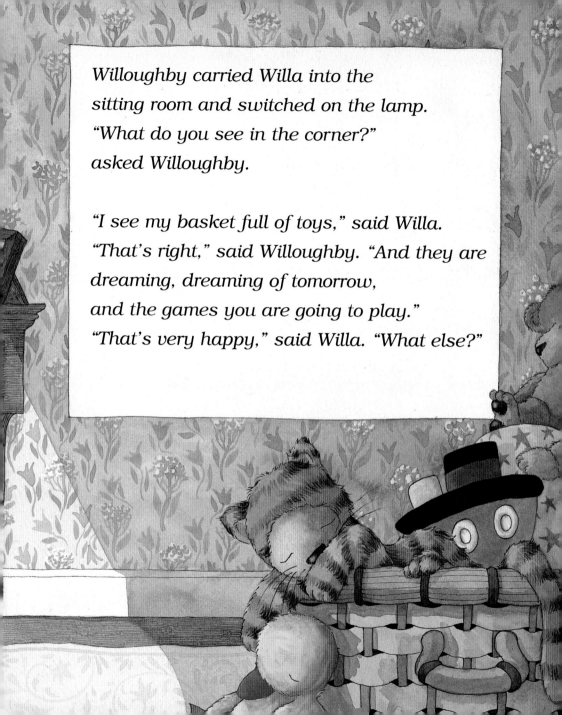

Willoughby carried Willa into the
sitting room and switched on the lamp.
"What do you see in the corner?"
asked Willoughby.

"I see my basket full of toys," said Willa.
"That's right," said Willoughby. "And they are
dreaming, dreaming of tomorrow,
and the games you are going to play."
"That's very happy," said Willa. "What else?"

Willoughby carried Willa to the window and opened the curtains wide. "What do you see in the darkness?" asked Willoughby.

"I see only the night," said Willa.
"Yes," said Willoughby. "And the night is waiting, waiting for the morning, which is on its way round the world."
"That's happy," said Willa.

"The morning is waiting too," said Willoughby. "What for?" said Willa. "Oh, lots of things," said Willoughby. "For flowers to bloom and clouds to float. For sun to shine and birds to fly. For bees to buzz and ducks to quack."

"That's a lot of happy things," said Willa.

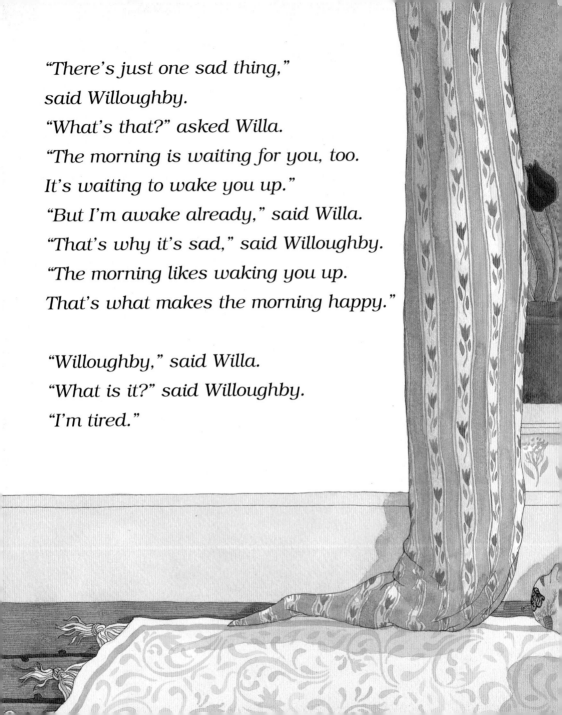

"There's just one sad thing,"
said Willoughby.
"What's that?" asked Willa.
"The morning is waiting for you, too.
It's waiting to wake you up."
"But I'm awake already," said Willa.
"That's why it's sad," said Willoughby.
"The morning likes waking you up.
That's what makes the morning happy."

"Willoughby," said Willa.
"What is it?" said Willoughby.
"I'm tired."

So Willoughby carried
Willa back to bed.
"What do you see in your
bed?" asked Willoughby.
"I see my ted," said Willa.
"And he's waiting for me to
snuggle up," said Willa.
"That's right," said
Willoughby, "waiting
especially for you."

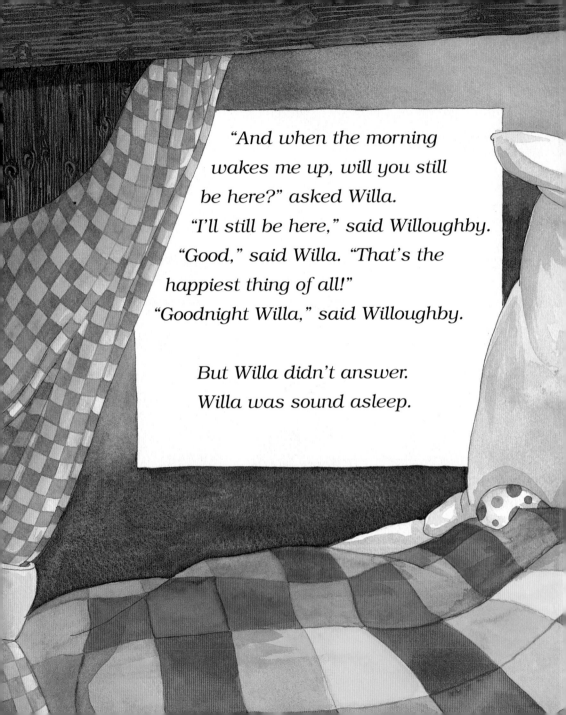

"And when the morning
wakes me up, will you still
be here?" asked Willa.
"I'll still be here," said Willoughby.
"Good," said Willa. "That's the
happiest thing of all!"
"Goodnight Willa," said Willoughby.

But Willa didn't answer.
Willa was sound asleep.

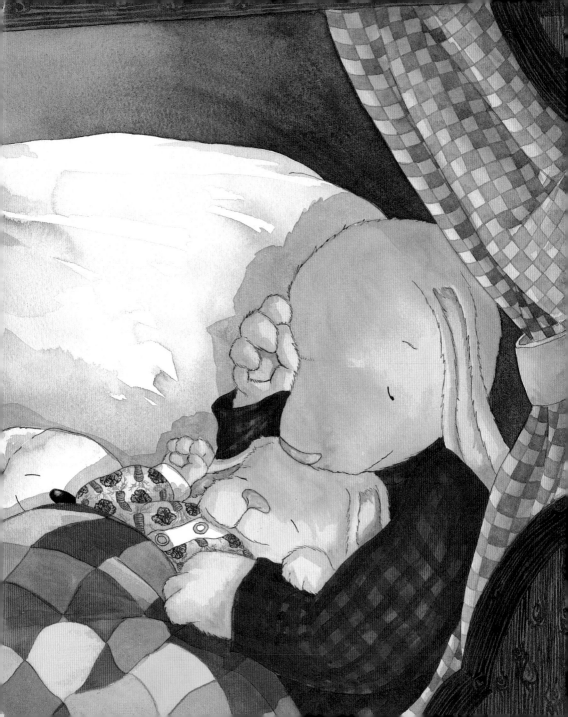